Ten on the Sled

ISBN 978-0-545-33103-6

Text copyright © 2010 by Kim Norman.
Illustrations copyright © 2010 by Liza Woodruff.
All rights reserved. Published by Scholastic Inc., 557 Broadway, New York, NY 10012,
by arrangement with Sterling Publishing Co., Inc. SCHOLASTIC and associated logos
are trademarks and/or registered trademarks of Scholastic Inc.

12 11 10 9 8 7 6 5 4 3 2 1   11 12 13 14 15 16/0

Printed in the U.S.A.   40

First Scholastic printing, January 2011

Designed by Kate Moll
The illustrations were created using
watercolor, colored pencil, and pastel.

For Collin and Skylar,
my two on the sled.
—K.N.

For Thomas and Edie.
—L.W.

Ten
on the
Sled

by
Kim
Norman

illustrated by
Liza
Woodruff

SCHOLASTIC INC.
New York Toronto London Auckland
Sydney Mexico City New Delhi Hong Kong

On a sunlit night,
'neath a snowy moon,
there was ONE on the sled,
then TWO, but soon . . .

There were TEN on the sled
and the caribou said,
"Slip over! Slide over!"
So they all slid over,

AAAAA

and Seal spilled out.

There were NINE on the sled
and the caribou said,
"It's snowing! Get going!"
So they all got going,

but Hare

hopped

out.

There were EIGHT on the sled
and the caribou said,
"It's slicker! Go quicker!"
So they all went quicker,

but Sheep shot out.

There were SEVEN on the sled
and the caribou said,
"We're gliding! Keep riding!"
So they all kept riding,

but Walrus

whirled out.

There were SIX on the sled
and the caribou said,
"We're lighter! Hold tighter!"
So they all held tighter,

but Fox flipped out.

There were FIVE on the sled
and the caribou said,
"Great thunder! Duck under!"
So they all ducked under,

but Squirrel

squeezed

out.

There were FOUR on the sled
and the caribou said,
"They're chasing! Keep racing!"
So they all kept racing,

but Wolf wiped out.

There were **THREE** on the sled
and the caribou said,
"They're winning! No spinning!"
So they all quit spinning,

but Moose

muddled out.

There were TWO on the sled
and the caribou said,
"Keep trying! We're flying!"
So they both kept flying,

till Bear bailed out.

There was ONE on the sled
and the caribou said,
"I'm only, I'm lonely,
I'm chilled to the bone.
A reindeer likes flying,
but never alone!"
So...

. . . ONE through TEN,
all leaped on again,
for one more run
and a little more fun
in the moonlit land
of the midnight sun.

THE END